east dragon, west dragon

For Rebekkah Storm Oliver, my favorite storyteller
—R. E.

For the Brodie kids: John, Ellie, and Max. I look forward to
hearing more of your stories.
—S. C.

ATHENEUM BOOKS FOR YOUNG READERS • An imprint of Simon & Schuster Children's Publishing Division • 1230 Avenue of the Americas, New York, New York 10020 • Text copyright © 2012 by Robyn Eversole • Illustrations copyright © 2012 by Scott Campbell • All rights reserved, including the right of reproduction in whole or in part in any form. • ATHENEUM BOOKS FOR YOUNG READERS is a registered trademark of Simon & Schuster, Inc. • For information about special discounts for bulk purchases, please contact Simon & Schuster Special Sales at 1-866-506-1949 or business@simonandschuster.com. • The Simon & Schuster Speakers Bureau can bring authors to your live event. For more information or to book an event, contact the Simon & Schuster Speakers Bureau at 1-866-248-3049 or visit our website at www.simonspeakers.com. • Book design by Sonia Chaghatzbanian • The text for this book is set in ITC Esprit. • The illustrations for this book are rendered in watercolor. • Manufactured in China • 1011 SCP • First Edition • 10 9 8 7 6 5 4 3 2 1 • Library of Congress Cataloging-in-Publication Data • Eversole, Robyn. • East Dragon, West Dragon / Robyn Eversole ; illustrated by Scott Campbell. — 1st ed. • p. cm. • Summary: East Dragon and West Dragon are suspicious of each other although they have never met, but when the western king is captured in the Eastern Kingdom and West Dragon goes to rescue him, they find they have much in common. • ISBN 978-0-689-85828-4 (hardcover) • ISBN 978-1-4169-8704-8 (eBook) • [1. Dragons—Fiction. 2. Prejudices—Fiction.] I. Campbell, Scott, 1973– ill. II. Title. • PZ7.E9235Eas 2012 • [E]—dc22 2010039609

east dragon, west dragon

story by Robyn Eversole   pictures by Scott Campbell

atheneum books for young readers • new york london toronto sydney new delhi

East Dragon
lived in
a palace.

West Dragon
lived in
a cave.

East Dragon had golden scales.

West Dragon was mossy green,
with brown splotches on his belly.

East Dragon and West Dragon lived on opposite sides of the world.

Of course, with West Dragon's big wings and East Dragon's long, swishy tail, crossing the sea was easy—but the two dragons never visited each other.

West Dragon thought East Dragon was a snob. East Dragon thought West Dragon was a slob.

And besides, being dragons, they were a little afraid of each other because they didn't know who was bigger, who was fiercer, and who had the bluest, hottest fire.

So they kept a world between them, just in case.

East Dragon lived with eight brothers and sisters—nine dragons in all.

The emperor liked having nine dragons in the palace for luck.

East Dragon liked the emperor, who was quiet, wise, and always took the excellent advice of dragons.

West Dragon didn't know any emperors.
He did know kings, though. Kings were a nuisance.
Kings kept knights. And knights were a bigger
nuisance. They barged into West Dragon's cave during
his naps, waving their silly swords.
Nothing made a cave smell nastier than roast knight.

Something had to be done. The knights had to go.
West Dragon rummaged around in his cave and
found a map.

It was an old map, the only one like it in the world.
He rolled it, sealed it, and gave it to the king.

The king unrolled the map. His knights came hurrying to look. They saw mountains and seas, treasures and quests, kingdoms and adventures.

They set off at once with jingling armor and swishing swords,

and West Dragon took a long, pleasant
nap that lasted through till January.

The king and his knights traveled far, far away and had hundreds of adventures. One day they arrived at a palace.

The emperor came out to greet them.

"Honorable King," he said graciously. "Welcome to our empire. Please stay for a visit."

The emperor ordered a feast. He hoped tin soldiers could eat.

Out came long, hot noodles and steaming plates of meat. The king and his knights ate lots.

Then they sat around the table and told the emperor grand stories, full of heroes and adventures, until the sun went down, the banquet hall grew dark . . .

and everything went wrong.

The emperor clapped his hands. "Enter," he said. The big doors swung open. Nine huge torches blazed, lighting up nine huge dragons.
The king stared. The knights stared.

"Dragons!" they cried. "ATTACK!"

Out came their swords.

The emperor frowned. He rang a small bell, and a few hundred imperial soldiers poured into the hall.

Soon the king and his knights were locked away in the dungeon, where they stayed all winter, shivering and grumbling and hungry and getting rather rusty, for the dungeon was damp.

Meanwhile, West Dragon woke up, yawned smokily, and looked for something to do. "Where are those silly knights?" he wondered.

When he flew over to the king's castle, he saw that it was deserted.

A messenger bird was circling. She had been circling a long time, because no one was home. When she saw West Dragon, she dropped a fat scroll on his tail.

It said:

To the Royal Chancellor,
if you have not gone
on holidays, or to
Anyone Else At All,

Help.

I'm being held
prisoner in the
Eastern Kingdom.
Do something
instantly!
~King

West Dragon sighed. Princes rescued princesses—at least, the ones who were too silly to rescue themselves. But who rescued silly kings?

Dragons, obviously.

West Dragon swooped into the air. With his huge wings, it was easy for him to cross all the mountains and seas, and drop down from the sky right into the emperor's gardens.

With his mossy green and brown skin, it was easy for him to slip unseen into the emperor's dungeon, burn through the doors with a fiery sneeze, and carry the king and all his knights safely away.

East Dragon looked up and saw West Dragon flying away with the king and all his knights.

"That dragon can fly!" he exclaimed. East Dragon could not fly.

He watched West Dragon up there among the clouds, and trembled. Then he hurried into the palace and hoped that big dragon would not come back.

As West Dragon flew out to sea, a ship full of pirates fired flaming arrows at him.

An arrow hit his wing. Ow! West Dragon spiraled toward the water. He yowled and yowled so loud that East Dragon heard from inside the palace, even with all the doors shut.

East Dragon slid over the courtyard wall. He slipped gracefully into the sea and swam out, his great golden tail beating up waves and overturning the pirate ship.

West Dragon was amazed.

"That dragon can swim!" he exclaimed. West Dragon could not swim.

He watched the long, shiny dragon and trembled, wishing he did not need rescuing.

East Dragon
brought
everyone
safely
to shore.

East Dragon and West Dragon looked at each other.

Each thought the other one was bigger and fiercer and had the bluest, hottest fire.

But when they made a bonfire to dry everyone off, they saw:

East Dragon's fire was not blue. It was glowy and golden.

West Dragon's fire was not blue either. It was warm and orange.

The two dragons stood side by side and found:

West Dragon was taller.

East Dragon was longer.

And neither one was very fierce.

So they looked at each other, smiled, and offered to take the king and his knights home in style, on the backs of **ten** leaping, diving, somersaulting dragons ...

to the king's castle for
a festive, friendly,
somewhat messy,
slightly rowdy,
long, dragon visit!